Meet Chopper.

Chopper is a droid.
A droid is a robot.

World of Reading

LEVEL 1

STAR WARS REBELS™

SEP 2016

ALWAYS BET ON CHOPPER

ADAPTED BY MEREDITH RUSU

BASED ON THE EPISODE "IDIOT'S ARRAY,"
WRITTEN BY KEVIN HOPPS

DISNEY
LUCASFILM PRESS
LOS ANGELES • NEW YORK

All rights reserved. Published by Disney • Lucasfilm Press, an imprint of Disney Book Group. No
part of this book may be reproduced or transmitted in any form or by any means, electronic or
mechanical, including photocopying, recording, or by any information storage and retrieval system,
without written permission from the publisher. For information address Disney • Lucasfilm Press,
1101 Flower Street, Glendale, California 91201.

Printed in the United States of America

First Edition, May 2015 10 9 8 7 6 5 4 3 2 1

Library of Congress Control Number: 2015931496

G658-7729-4-15079

ISBN 978-1-4847-0560-5

Visit the official *Star Wars* website at: www.starwars.com

Chopper helps the rebels.
He is good at fixing things.

Zeb is Chopper's friend.
Zeb likes to play cards.

One day, Zeb played cards
with a man named Lando.

Zeb bet Lando he could win!

Zeb wanted fuel if he won.
Lando wanted Chopper if
he won.

Zeb did not win.
Chopper was very angry!

Lando offered the rebels a deal.

Lando needed help sneaking
a secret box to Lothal.

If the rebels helped him,
he would give them fuel.

And he would give Chopper back.

The rebels agreed to help Lando.

Zeb felt bad about the
card game.

He told Chopper he
was sorry.

Chopper was still angry.

He pretended to be friends
with Lando instead!

That made Zeb angry, too.
He and Ezra opened
Lando's secret box.

Inside was a puffer pig!

The pig escaped.
Zeb and Ezra chased it.

It was so scared that it
puffed up like a balloon!

Lando found them.
He explained that the pig would
sniff out treasure on Lothal.

Lando would be rich.

The rebels flew to Lothal.

But they were attacked
by mean thugs!

Lando owed the thugs money.

Chopper and the rebels
helped Lando fight the thugs.

The puffer pig helped, too.

The rebels won!

The thugs left . . . quickly.

Lando thanked the rebels.

He gave Chopper back.

But he did not give them
fuel!

Lando was sneaky.

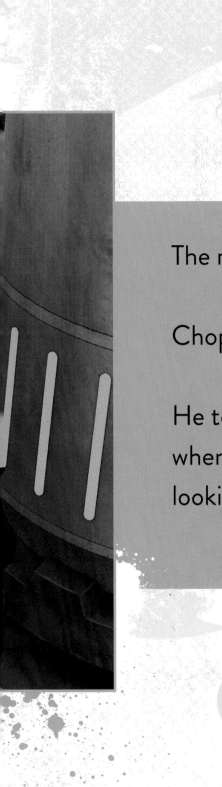

The rebels left.

Chopper was sneaky, too.

He took a barrel of fuel when Lando was not looking.

Chopper is very good
at fixing problems.

The rebels can
always bet on Chopper!